D0904267

We begin by lighting sage to purify our hearts,

and through the dancing movement of the smoke, we weave story and vision to create a sacred ceremony. . . .

We call this ceremony STORIES OF THE DREAMWALKERS.

MI TAKUYE OYACIN . . .

To All My Relations . . . In Heart and Spirit

printed in u.s.a.

Library of Congress Catalog Card No. 89-062733

isbn 0-944082-01-7

this book was published by
Santa Fe Fine Arts Publishing, Ltd.
Santa Fe, New Mexico

Stories of the Dreamwalkers

by
Joyce Mills and Frank Howell

text
Joyce Mills
images
Frank Howell
design
Daniel Bish

Table of Contents

Whistling Wind and Singing Breeze

It was a cool evening during the Budding Trees Moon of Spring. The gentle breezes were singing their harmonious melodies, as the shadows of the soft, white clouds blanketed the deep valleys of the mighty mountains.

The flames danced within the crackling campfire as the young eyes listened eagerly while the Silver-haired One began to weave another of her medicine stories . . . .

A long time ago, when the earth had tall grass and blue skies, there were two Spirit Mates of Nature known as Whistling Wind and Singing Breeze. Through the blending of their melodies, they sang their message of harmony and peace to the four sacred directions for all creatures of Mother Earth to hear and appreciate.

One night, as the two Spirit Mates rested deep in the heart of their mountain, Singing Breeze had a dream . . . not just an ordinary dream but a dream of Vision in which she

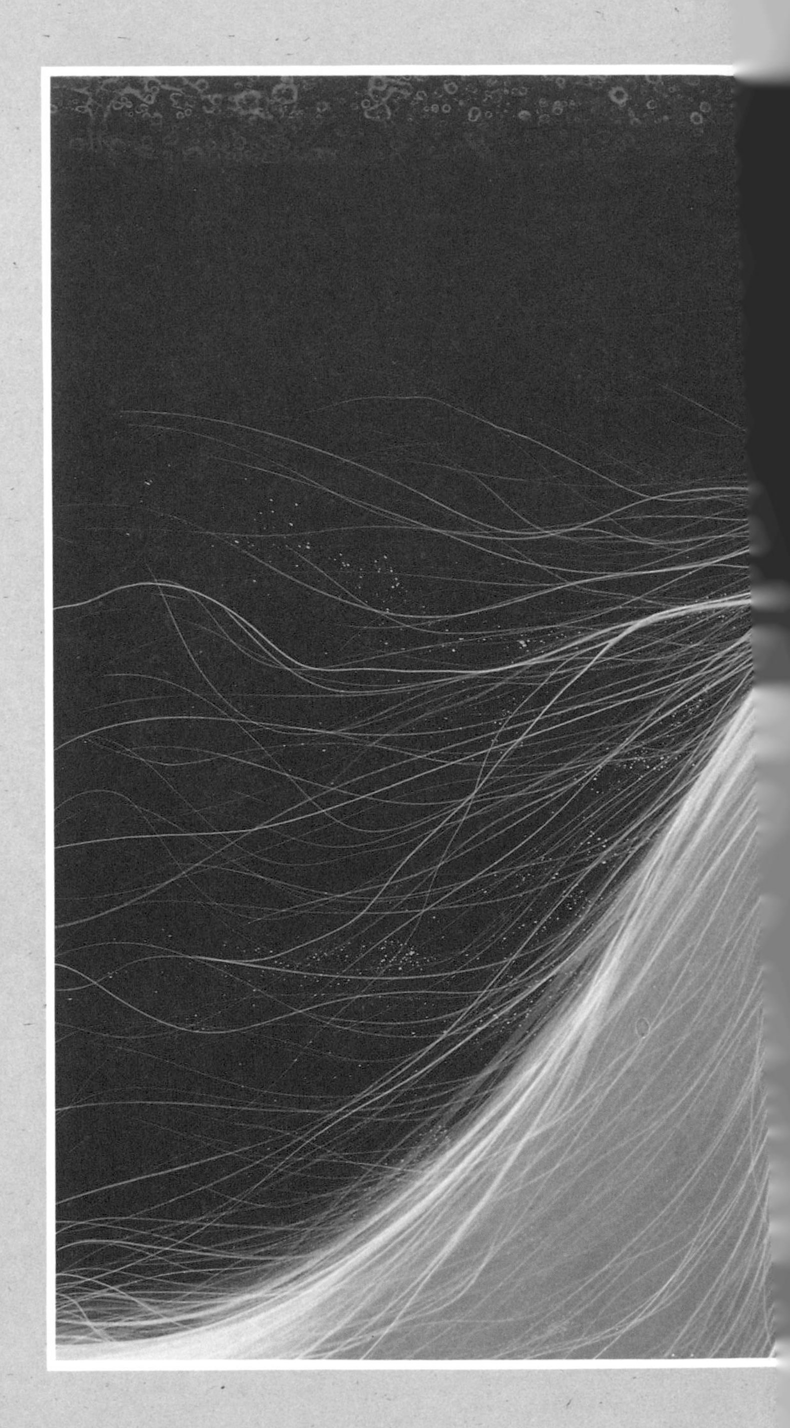

saw a dark shadow coming to try and take the light of her peace melody. The Vision Dream showed her a path and told her to follow quickly, for it was at the end of this path that she would find what she needed to protect the light of her melody.

"This is your journey. . . your personal quest. . . you must follow alone."

For the first time throughout their lifetimes together, she had to journey without her mate. It was a task of great difficulty for her to do, yet she knew the message of the Vision Dream was important. . . she knew she had to do this alone.

During this same night, while Whistling Wind dreamed of his beloved Singing Breeze and of their many wondrous adventures, he awoke with a suddenness and an uneasy feeling within his center. He looked about, but Singing Breeze was gone. Whistling Wind began calling to his Spirit Mate, but the air remained quiet except for the sound of his echo. He whistled their favorite nature melody, but still the mountains were quiet. There was no sign of Singing Breeze, his beloved friend of many lifetimes.

Whistling Wind was desperately seeking Vision help to find his mate. It seemed that, even though he could not hear her, he sensed her presence. . . and felt a looming danger.

Lifting his presence high into the night sky of many stars, Whistling Wind sent his searching melody down deep within the mighty forests. . . down through the branches and limbs of each tree, deeply to the roots within Mother Earth. Still, there was only silence in the air.

After many hours, Whistling Wind grew tired and went back to the heart of the mountain to rest. The colorful leaves swirled gently as he stirred in his own little place.

During the fourth night of his search for his beloved mate, Whistling Wind was gently awakened by something familiar fluttering about. After a moment he recognized his little brother, Blue Feather. He began telling Whistling Wind that while he was flying about he had heard a new, yet familiar, melody through veils of water by the sacred stream . . . . "Maybe it is Singing Breeze."

Whistling Wind felt hope in his heart when he heard this. Blue Feather fluttered his wings, calling for his brother to follow . . .

and so, gathering up all of his energy as winds do, finding his center, up he went with Blue Feather to find the gentle Singing Breeze.

Blue Feather guided him to the shadowed canyons, along the many red clay paths and down to the white flowing rivers.

"Look," said Blue Feather with excitement in his voice, "There are the veils of water. It is the waterfall of the sacred stream." As they moved closer, they began to hear the different, yet familiar, melody. The sound seemed to radiate from deep within the caverns behind the falling water. Blue Feather excitedly flew about, pointing the way for Whistling Wind to follow.

There he saw his beloved Spirit Mate singing her song of Peace with a new power and energy. Whistling Wind sent his gentle love Voice to his mate to let her know he was there. When Singing Breeze heard this familiar sound, she felt a swirling warmness inside her center. They embraced in joyful reunion. . . while Blue Feather flew off, deeply satisfied, knowing his relations were united once again.

"My heart was filled with great worry," Whistling Wind told Singing Breeze. "I thought I had lost you forever."

Singing Breeze surrounded him with her gentleness while she spoke of the great dream of Vision in which she was shown a dark shadow coming to try and take her melody of peace.

"I had to follow this path to its end to discover what I need to protect my peace melody. The Vision Dream told me that this is my personal quest and that I must journey alone. I left quickly because of the great danger."

Whistling Wind listened as his mate continued with her full breath.

"I travelled many long hours on the path, not knowing where I was going, feeling afraid. I travelled until I felt I could travel no more. . . yet I continued still. After the moon had come up four times, I came to this place where we stand together now. . . and somehow I knew this was where I was to spend alone time. It is a sacred place of rediscovery. It is the place for me to again remember the true and powerful message of my Peace Melody. For once I was able to remember, I knew the light would be safe again. I know now that the power of the light lies in the memory of the True Message."

Whistling Wind listened with proudness to the story of his Spirit Mate. He knew that by following the path shown to her by her Vision Dream she had done a brave thing.

Whistling Wind and Singing Breeze stayed together in this place, enjoying their time of reuniting. When it was time, they returned to the heart of their sacred mountain to once again blend their melodies of Peace and Harmony to the four directions, for all the creatures of the Mother to hear and appreciate.

The young eyes were now in the world of dreams, and the flames in the campfire danced smaller steps, as the Silver-haired One ended her story by whispering. . . .

"The power of the light lies in the memory of the True Message."

Dancing Butterflies

■ ■ ■ The air was moist and warm as the dark-haired woman journeyed on the road of red earth that wound its way up into the mountains. Her mind was filled with many searching questions as she carefully followed the directions that she had been given . . . each step bringing her closer to the lodge of Two Suns, the man of the medicine ways. She had never travelled this path before . . . it was new to her; yet, somehow she knew inside that this was to be a meeting of great importance . . . a meeting of great spirit learning.

After what seemed to be many hours of winding roads, the woman came to the turnoff point which she had been directed to take. She followed this road a short distance until she came to the place of meeting. Protected by tall trees of pine and cedar, the lodge was nestled far off the main road. It was a place of small colorful gardens growing both food and flowers with many young animals scampering about. She could feel her heart beating fast within her breast as she looked about for Two Suns and called his name.

As gracefully as the sun rises in the east to greet the day, he appeared from behind the lodge and greeted her with his warm, bright one-tooth-missing smile. "I'm happy to be here," she said, and gave him the tobacco-offering she had been carrying in her large straw sack. His soft brown eyes twinkled in the sunlight as he accepted her gift with an open heart. "Let us talk there," he said, pointing to a place a few feet away overlooking the gardens. Without hesitation she agreed. Just as they got settled, soft warm drops of rain began to fall from the clouded sky. She wondered if they should go inside.

At the same moment she began her wondering, he looked up and with a clear strong voice said, "This is good, this meeting is blessed." Her heart felt a private smile as she agreed in the quiet space of her mind, "Yes, this is good."

His full attention was with her as she began to speak. "This is a time of changing paths for me. . . a time of wanting to know more. . . of quest, yet of great confusion." Tears were beginning to come to her eyes as she spoke.

He was puffing his tobacco while he listened. Glancing out at the garden to gather her thoughts, she noticed two small white butterflies fluttering about a few feet from where they sat and called them to his attention. Still puffing his tobacco, he smiled and said, "Yes, and keep watching for there are two more coming. . . and two more. . . and two more." After a few moments, the garden was filled with small white butterflies magically dancing before them.

She smiled with childlike delight as she sat entranced watching these delicate creatures of nature paint a message of graceful movement in flight.

Still puffing on his tobacco, this medicine man of quiet wisdom continued talking to her by saying, "Remember to look beyond that which is ordinary; for if you do not, you will only see the white wings of the butterfly. Learn to look beyond what you see with your everyday eyes and see the full cycle of her dance. See with the full vision of your heart, and it will always guide you towards the path of true spirit learning. . . towards your true direction."

She listened and absorbed his words with her full presence.

Many suns have risen and set since that time in the garden of spirit learning, yet her memories are full and fresh. . . and the butterflies still dance, bringing vision in many different ways.

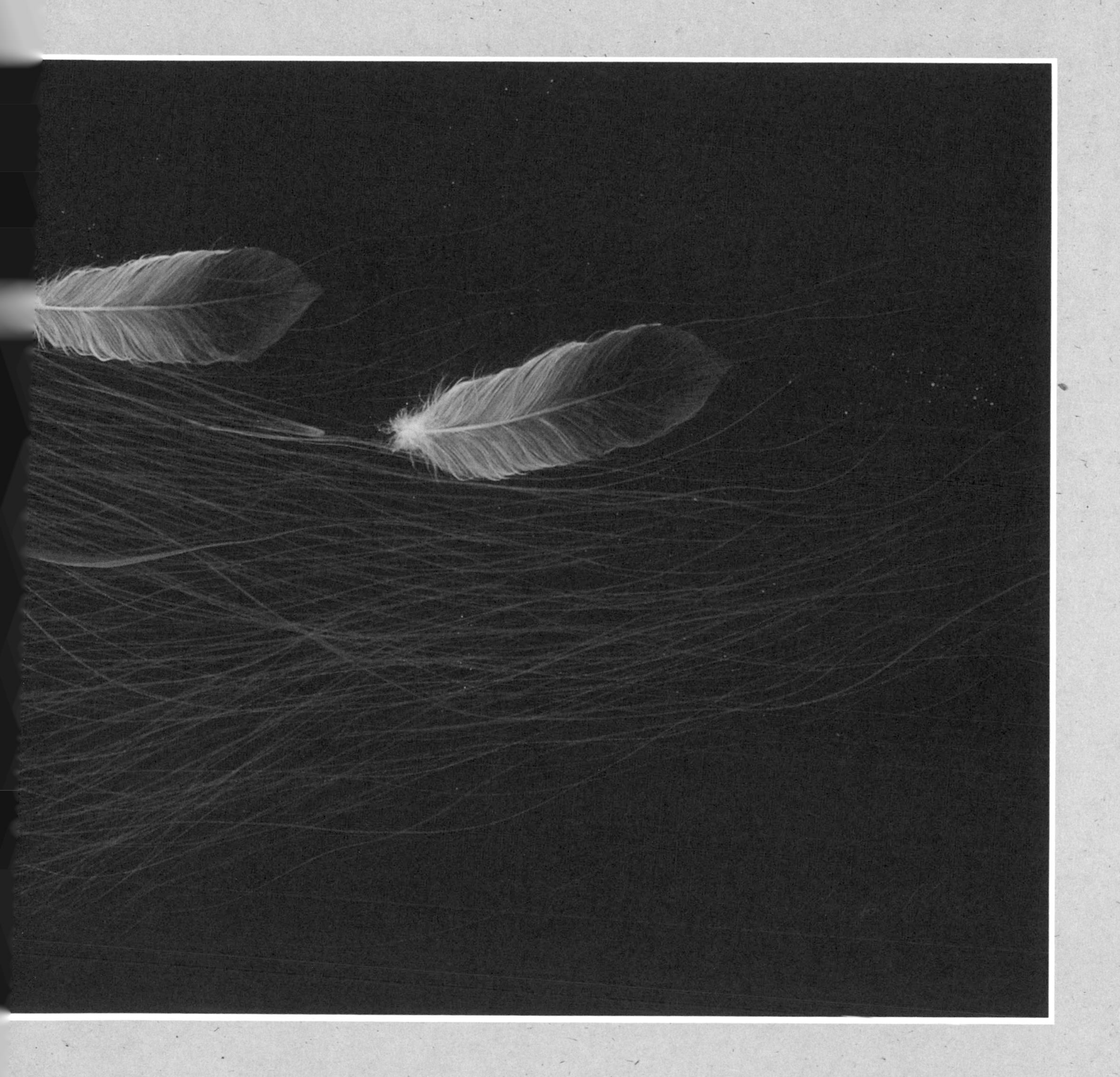

Eagle of the Sea

He was a tall, slender young man with smooth copper-tanned skin that shimmered in the sunlight. His body was strong with sculptured muscles and his face looked as if it had been chiseled by a master craftsman, reflecting fine lines and high cheekbones. His eyes were soft and dark as they spoke words of a quiet spirit. . . . On the island of flowers, he was known as Eagle of the Sea.

It was a day of strong breezes, as the deep turquoise blue water glistened from the sun's reflective rays.

The woman watched as he skillfully readied their small vessel for the sail. Her heart began to beat rapidly as the time drew nearer and the winds became stronger. Inside she felt a wave of fear weaving within her flame of excitement . . . . It was to be her first time on an adventure such as this.

Sensing her apprehension, he looked at her with eyes of dark pearls and motioned for her to come closer. "We are almost ready," he said with quiet assurance. "Watch me carefully, as I am going to push the vessel into the water very slowly. When I give the signal, we will have to lift our bodies quickly onto the canvas, for the winds are strong and will swiftly carry us out to sea."

Her body's movement was as swift and bold as the ocean's waves. Without a thinking thought in her mind, she found herself placed just where she was supposed to be. This woman of new adventure held on tightly to the ropes that were on either side of her, balancing her body with the powerful motion that moved beneath their sail. His eyes were focused and his body firmly positioned as he guided the vessel through the fast-moving waves toward the open sea.

His long fingers caressed the lines as she continued watching this young guide open his colorful wings of sail to capture the full breath of the wind. His movements were graceful and sure as he worked the lines with a natural ease. Truly he was a master of the ocean . . . a bird of spirit in flight . . . an EAGLE OF THE SEA.

After what seemed to be a timeless time, she began to feel a question stirring deep within . . . . "How do you know when it is time to change directions?" she asked. With his quick-moving hands still working the ropes of the sail, he looked deeply into her eyes and responded with a whispery yet strong voice, "You watch the sail and feel the wind, and you just know inside when it is time to change."

Throughout the day of sailing, his words continued to resonate deeply within the center of her being . . . . "You watch the sail and feel the wind, and you just know inside when it is time to change."

She knew that she had received a most treasured gift . . . and she thanked him.

The early morning was clear as she sat on the soft green blanket of Mother Earth and felt the dry heat of the desert sun caress her coppery tanned skin. On this morning she cradled a Pipe of Prayer in her arms and began to hear its voice talk to her.

"I am yours now. I have been given to you by the medicine woman known as Starfire. I spoke through her voice last night and chose, among all the others, to be with you. Starfire has taken me to many sacred ceremonies. I have been blessed many times. It is now you who will carry me and bring honor to my name."

GIVE-AWAY

The voice of the Pipe was strong and proud.

She closed her eyes and let her mind drift back to the memories of the night before. . . to the memories of the woman known as Starfire. . . ceremony. . . sage. . . talking circle. . . and GIVE-AWAY.

Carefully spreading her cloth with delicately flowered embroidery gracing each of the four corners, Starfire slowly began to place many sacred treasures of both earth and spirit before her. With her dark eyes glistening, she leaned forward to light the sage nesting within the pearl center of a hand-sized abalone shell. Fragrance and smoke quickly began to swirl through the air as she fluttered the Spirit

Eagle Feather about each of her Sisters present. Starfire then handed the Feather and shell of sage to the gentle-faced woman on her left and motioned for her to do the same. . . . The ceremonial purification had begun.

Starfire carefully lifted a Sacred Pipe which was resting on the cloth before her. With the melody of flute playing in the background, she told the story of how White Buffalo Cow Woman had come to the Lakota people long ago and had given them the gift of the Sacred Pipe. With the voice of a strong flowing river she said, "All those who smoke the Pipe are joined as one breath with the Universe."

Starfire then stood with the Pipe in her hands and offered it to Grandfather Spirit, Grandmother Earth, and the Four Sacred Directions. Her lips touched the wooden stem as she inhaled gently the ceremonial tobacco. With a swirling motion, she passed the Pipe to her Sister on her left.

Each woman present took her turn inhaling the breath of many ancestors while offering prayer.

When the Pipe had gone full circle, returning to its keeper, Starfire placed it down gently before her once again. She then picked up the Spirit Eagle Feather and began the Talking Circle. Each woman held the Feather and spoke of private stories from within her heart. The circle grew closer in spirit as the stories unfolded. MI TAKUYE OYACIN, sacred words meaning TO ALL MY RELATIONS, were spoken by each woman after she completed her story and was ready to pass the Feather.

Like the Pipe, after the Feather had been passed full circle, it was returned to its special place on the cloth.

The woman known as Starfire began to tell her Sisters that she was feeling a GIVE-AWAY. She reminded those present that in the Native American way, it is believed that we do not own anything, but are simply the keepers of the many treasures of the Universe. She said that since we are only the keepers of those treasures, we must let them go when it is time. . . . WE MUST GIVE THEM AWAY.

Starfire lifted yet another Pipe, with clay bowl and feathers of white gracefully hanging from its wooden stem. With words of strength she said, "During ceremony tonight this Pipe has spoken in full voice and has told me it is time for me to give it away to another who will continue to honor its Sacred Power and meaning."

Looking deeply into the eyes of the dark-haired woman sitting across from her, she leaned forward, placed the Pipe in her hands, and with love embracing her words she said, "It now belongs to you. Listen to its voice and see the many visions it will bring to you." Her Sister of many lifetimes trembled and cried as she accepted this most sacred of gifts.

"I do not yet know its full sacred power and meaning. I am but a child in the early stages of learning. But I do know that, like the sun to a flowering bud, the petals of learning will unfold as I bring the great warmth of honor to this Pipe."

Starfire nodded, reflecting a quiet pleasure of an inner knowing.

◆ ◆ ◆

The air was still quiet as her mind returned to the dry desert morning. Upon opening her eyes, she saw her new gift still cradled in her arms. . . . And as the rivers flow full after a warm rain, she felt the fullness of honor flowing deeply within her heart.

Silently she gave thanks, whispering the words MI TAKUYE OYACIN . . . TO ALL MY RELATIONS.

It had been a cool evening with light rain that brought the forest a thin blanket of frost.

CIRCLE

The morning sun was just beginning to spread wings of warmth over the mighty trees and through the sprawling bushes,

OF

creating a melting symphony of crystal sounds.

TRANSFORMATION

How privileged the woman felt in her heart to be included in such a special concert of nature.

It was a day she had set aside to gather wild flowers and healing herbs. . . . As she walked, she began to feel a familiar presence by her side. When she looked around, she saw a little bird of grey and white feathers following her. Pausing for a moment, she smiled and said, "Hello Grandmother, it has been a long time since I have felt your Spirit."

Her Grandmother had gone to the other side many years before; yet, from time to time, her powerful Spirit would visit her beloved Granddaughter. . . . This was one of those times.

"Grandmother, I have missed you. . . . It is good to see you once again. I have done much growing since I last saw you. I am a **woman** now, not just a girl."

"Ahhh," whispered the Grandmother, "so you think you are a **woman** now. Tell me, then, what has become of the girl?"

"I do not know," answered the Granddaughter. "I think she has gone far away to the place of children."

Upon hearing those words, Grandmother said, "Come with me, my Granddaughter, I have something to show you." Together, they journeyed along a narrow path which led through the cool-breezed forest, passing the huge old cedar trees of great wisdom, the many young pine trees with their fresh fragrances, and the always changing manzanita trees along the way.

With her Granddaughter following closely behind, the little bird of grey and white feathers flew over to a place of many great brownish-red colored rocks.

"Look over there—look deep into that open space within the forest," Grandmother said.

Granddaughter turned her head and looked where her Spirit Grandmother was flying. There, in the middle of the open space, was a tree stump of great size. She could tell that at one time, this was a wise and mighty tree of great knowing. Granddaughter walked closer and saw that the inside of the tree stump was hollowed. . . . As if the wind were speaking she heard her Grandmother whisper, "Become the tree." She let the words of her Spirit Grandmother echo softly in her mind. . . . "Become the Tree." After pausing for a few quiet moments, she decided to climb inside the mighty stump and let the tree talk to her.

When comfortably inside, Granddaughter closed her eyes, took a deep breath, and felt the body of the tree with her hands. Soon she felt her body becoming tall and straight . . . reaching for the sun . . . hearing the sounds of the forest . . . feeling the coolness of the protective branches and limbs surrounding this new image of her body. . .

She began to see through the eyes of the

tree. . . . It was a quiet reflective time. As if the petals of a flower were unfolding, a vision memory began to reveal itself. . . a vision memory of the many squirrel families playing on her branches and limbs. She remembered feeling strong and protective as they stored their food deep inside her trunk for the cold storm times of the Winter. . . and the memory transformed into a vision of many birds building their nests. . . preparing for their new families of little winged ones. . . . And she remembered the leaves of many sizes that appeared on her branches through the changing seasons.

Many hours passed before Granddaughter opened her eyes and returned to her full awareness.

"Come, let us walk further. Let us wander down this path through the forest to the Stream of Before," Grandmother said.

"The Stream of Before," her Granddaughter wondered to herself, "What is that?" "Just follow," Grandmother said, "just follow and save your questions."

Granddaughter laughed to herself and did as her Grandmother suggested.

"Now, look deeply into this stream and see your reflection as I talk to you. Earlier today, my beloved Granddaughter, you said that you are a woman now, not a child. . . that is but a half truth; for in order to be a true woman, you must first embrace the girl-child within. She has not gone away. . . she is just present in another form. Your child spirit is a crystal essence. . . an essence which empowers your woman spirit to feel life and energy. Remember, the circle of transformation is complete when the flower has danced from seed to bud, from bud to full opening, returning from full opening to the beginning seed once again."

When Grandmother finished her words, Granddaughter noticed a curious thing. The reflection she had been looking at had changed. It was familiar, yet different. . . . It was the reflection of a child. . . and the child was her from a long time ago. . . .

The Child and the Woman spent many hours together, reacquainting themselves once again. . . the Child with the Woman and Woman with the Child. . . . It was an important time, it was a good time. The Woman reached her hand into the stream and drew some cool water into her mouth. "I did not realize how thirsty I have been. Thank you for reminding me."

It was time for the Woman to return home.
She looked around to say good-bye once again to her Grandmother, but the little bird was gone . . . .
All that remained beside the Stream of Before was a nest . . .
a nest with a few grey and white feathers resting within its center.

As the Woman wandered back on the path through the forest returning home,
she realized that she had forgotten to gather the wild flowers and healing herbs that she set out to gather earlier that morning . . .
or had she?

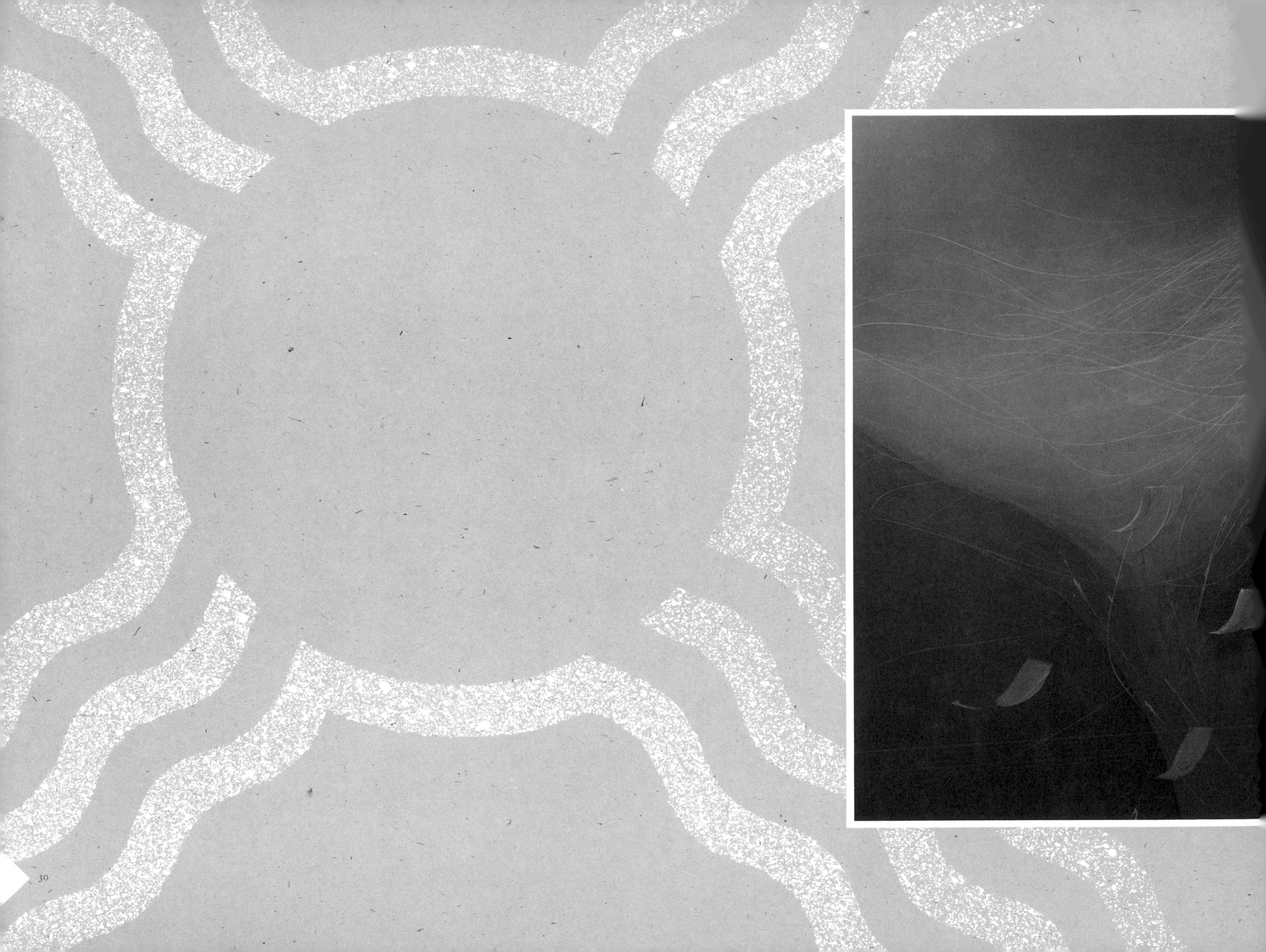

THE SUN DANCE

The heat of the late afternoon sun in July was still strong, as the woman with flowing dark hair walked through the forest gathering wood for her evening campfire. She felt a deep sense of contentment within each of her steps as she wandered happily about, stopping to pick up small dried twigs and large branches.

As she was following a narrow curved path that was rich with much of the wood she needed, the woman came face to face with a tall, large-framed man with hair of long black braids. His face was soft and round with high rosy-bronzed cheekbones and his eyes smiled in the sunlight.

"Hello," he said, while reaching his hand toward her in greeting.

"Hello," she replied with a warm smile, extending her hand to meet his. As they touched, she felt a sense of surprise wave through her body. "Hmmmm," she thought to herself, "for such a large man, his touch is so very soft and gentle, it is like that of a baby's warm skin."

Looking into his eyes, she saw a penetrating peacefulness resting within his soul's message. There was a moment of connectedness that had transpired between them as quickly as a firefly flashes her light in the darkness of a warm summer night.

Without saying another word, they parted. She continued gathering her wood, and was not aware of giving the meeting any further thought. However, throughout the evening, the feeling of his touch seemed to return . . . and she did not know why.

The camp was busy with many families settling in for the activities of the days to follow. Campfires were blazing, children were laughing, and there were the delighted voices of friends and relatives being reunited after many years.

That night, as she lay in the darkness under the sweet-smelling pine trees, the songs of her wolf brothers and sisters could be heard throughout the camp. Somehow their songs became a lullaby, and she fell deeply asleep.

When she was in the place of deep dreaming, the presence of a much-loved brother of her tribe came to her.

"My Sister," he said, "when the drumming begins, you will be lost in the movement of the Dance. . . you will be transported to a time of long ago. . . a time of the Great Buffalo. . . when the waters were clean and the air was like the sweet breath of a baby. . . and you will dance."

"You will dance in support of all the Dancers. . . the Dancers who come to this great arbor, to the sacred tree, and dance for the peace of all the peoples of our Earth, and you will become one with each of them in a special way. . . . And during the Sun Dance, you will be touched in ways that you have not ever been touched before. When the four days of the Sun Dance are over and all is silent, you will leave this place. You will know that you have been touched forever in your heart, and you will never be able to see the things of life in the same way. But, my Sister, there may be one Dancer who will become a partner. . . a partner of a different kind. . . a partner you may never know other than here in the Sun Dance; yet, you will dance together in the way of a silent spirit forever."

The words of her tribal brother stayed with her throughout her time of dreaming. After what seemed to be a long night of journey, the woman was awakened by sounds of the eagle-bone whistles signalling for the Sun Dance to begin.

The many people of the camp gathered in the branch-covered arbor. In its center stood the great sacred tree representing the center of the universe. The sounds of the mighty drums were like the heartbeat of the Earth, and the voices of those chanting were like the strongest song of the wind. With wreaths of sage surrounding their heads, the Dancers began to enter the great arbor through the East with all the beauty and magnitude of a strong, flowing river. All the Dancers carried Sacred Pipes cradled within their arms. The Dancers were of old years, of middle years, and of young years. They were men and they were women . . . they were boys and they were girls. . . . The woman knew her eyes were being honored by seeing the most beautiful of dances . . . the most sacred of ceremonies . . . the Sun Dance.

The Dancers would dance in the blazing sun without food, without water, for four days. . . . They would participate in sweatlodge ceremonies twice a day to keep their spirits pure. . . . They would dance until their feet and bodies could endure no more and then they would continue, because of their commitment to the Sustenance of Life. But this was just the first day . . . the day of the beginning.

One by one, the Dancers began to come forward and offer their greatest gift . . . the gift of their flesh for the survival of the

Earth. . . . And then she saw him, the man with the warm smile and tender touch of the day before. There he was being fastened to the great sacred tree in the center of the arbor. . . bonded by a rope attached to the two small stakes that were pierced through his flesh. . . bonded as an unborn child is bonded to the womb of its mother by the cord of life. . . . He danced with the power and brightness of the Sun. . . and he would dance until his flesh tore loose. . . until he was born into freedom.

Throughout the four days, he stayed tied to the sacred tree. . . and throughout the four days, she danced and chanted in support. This combination of gentle man and powerful warrior showed no awareness of her. . . . He was in a deeper trance that transcended the presence of outside reality. . . until the moment finally came. . . . He pulled back and released himself with a shrill cry of joy! When he was free, he, along with many supporters, circled the arbor and, then, in an unexpected moment of connectedness, his eyes met hers once again and sent a quiet message of appreciation. For the moment, it was a relationship of a different kind. It was not like that of a man and woman who share their bodies. . . it was a bonding on the level of spirit. . . in this time. . . in this place. . . in this moment.

The vision of his warm smile and the feeling of his gentle touch were being woven into her memory forever.

Long into the night, after the ceremonial feast brought closure to the last four days of the Sun Dance, she lay beneath the stars feeling like she had passed through a lifetime. She wondered if she was, perhaps, still in the place of deep dreaming. . . . Had she really met the man with the long black braids, warm smile, and gentle touch—or had it all been a dream . . .? Or, perhaps, she wondered, had she entered his place of deep dreaming. . . had she entered a dream of his?

The Dreamspeaker

■ ■ ■ Great darkness fell within as the final flap was lowered over the entrance of the sacred sweatlodge, erasing the last glint of outside light. The deeply flowing voice of the leader began to sing songs of purification and prayer, as he sprinkled cedar over each of the red-glowing Grand-father rocks which rested in the center of the lodge. As he slowly poured the water over each of the rocks, they became even more powerful, taking on a presence deeply felt by each person in the circle.

Feeling the intense fear building within her heart as the steam embraced her body, she wanted desperately to escape. . . but she knew that she must not break this circle. She felt herself losing complete control as the heat continued to envelop all of her thinking power.

As if the voice of the wind were speaking to her, the words of the leader swirled

through the darkness and heat.

"Breathe deeply four times and stay with your prayers. It is only from your fear that you wish to run." He continued, "The Grandfathers are your relatives, they are here to protect you . . . to teach you. Stay and look deeply into each of them for guidance and comfort."

She did as the leader told her to do—she breathed deeply as her heart continued its rapid drumming within her chest. After what seemed to be a lifetime of time, her breathing began to slow down and her heart became rhythmic once again. Just as she felt her strength returning, a vision of a powerful mountain began to reveal itself from within the pulsing heart of the mighty Grandfather rock glowing before her in the darkness. The mountain vision that she was seeing did not have trees but, instead, had the greenness of cedar resting on its peak. In the mist-filled darkness, the prayers and songs continued and her vision became stronger. Somehow, the piercing heat was not felt with the same burning strength. The mountain vision spoke to her in ways she had not heard before in her lifetime.

When the fourth round of the sweatlodge ceremony was completed, she stepped into the light once again. As she emerged, she wondered, "But what of this vision? What does this mean?" She wondered . . . but she did not know.

A young, long-haired man, who tended the fire for the rocks, saw the glazed look in her round dark eyes as she gathered her thoughts outside of the sweatlodge.

"Do you want to talk a bit?" he asked. She told him of her intense feeling of fear that transformed into a vision of a great mountain . . . a mountain she had seen emerge from within the glow of the Grandfather Rock. Knowing that she had experienced something important, this young man of the fire suggested that she talk to someone in the camp known as an interpreter, a Dreamspeaker. Although still confused, the woman felt a gratefulness within her heart for his suggestion.

Later that afternoon, while she sat with her friend sharing stories of the day, a stocky man with long gray hair blowing from the breath of the wind appeared in their camp. She knew this was the man she had been directed to meet . . . . This was the man known as the Dreamspeaker.

He looked off into the distance for a long moment before he spoke. "I heard you had a vision that you want to know more about," he said. "Tell me what it was that you saw." The woman openly told of her time in the sweatlodge and of how the mountain vision had come to her within the glow of the Great Rock.

Still gazing off, the Dreamspeaker then told her, "This is not a vision of today, it is a vision of the future. . . of tomorrow. It is not a mountain as we know it, but it appears to be a volcano." As he spoke, the wind grew stronger as if echoing the words of this man of vision.

Her mind drifted to images of a far-away island of deep blue waters, powerful cliffs and vibrant flowers. . . . She thought about the strong feeling erupting inside her of wanting to share much with others.

The Dreamspeaker continued, "There are many ways to see a vision . . . many ways to hear a story. I can only tell you my way of seeing. It is for you to seek its true and full teaching with great slowness and patience. Remember, the Spirit reveals only a tiny bit of vision at a time."

While many meanings danced within the shadows of the woman's mind, she was content not to have any answers at all . . . and yet to have all of the answers in the colors of more questions.

It was the time of sunset when ribbons of fiery colors danced their magic through the evening sky. While the woman sat high on a sacred cliff gazing out towards the ocean's horizon, the blue surf pounded its mystical symphony below. Her mind was focused on a faraway place across the blue pacific waters. . . a place where her little sister had been struggling for a long time with a great darkness within her delicate body. The river of her breath was growing weaker as she was getting closer to making her journey to the world of many ancestors. . . the world of spirit.

Deer Sister

It was on this night that the woman knew many relatives were gathering in a sacred meeting to help her sister make the journey one of beauty, peace and comfort.

Wanting so much to be there, yet being so far away, the woman felt a deep sadness within her heart. Through the many tears streaming from her eyes, a vision came to her of her little sister and of the many faces of her relatives all sitting in the sacred meeting of all-night prayer.

As the vision became clearer, a story came to her mind. . . a story for her little sister so far away.

"Please Grandfather Wind, carry this story to my sister," she prayed. "Carry this story so she will know I am with her."

As if all of the Grandfathers had heard her request, a great Wind began to blow with a powerful force. Knowing her prayers had been answered, she took a breath and began . . . .

A long time ago, when the forests were full with the grandmother and grandfather trees, there was a little deer of great beauty. All the creatures of this forest knew her as Little Flower because of her petal-soft features. Little Flower always had one curiosity. She wondered, "How did the moon become white?" She would ask her relatives of the forest, but all they would say was, "Some day when the time is right, you will know." Little Flower would walk away, still confused. She wanted to know the answer to her question.

One day, as she was going about her daily business, Little Flower came upon a great white feather and knew that it belonged to her relative, White Eagle Mother. "Hmm," she thought to herself, "if I keep this feather, perhaps I, too, will have some of White Eagle Mother's power to see in many directions. Perhaps one day I will find out about the moon."

Little Flower tucked the feather away within the fur of her light brown coat and kept walking until the white moon was

glowing brightly in the dark sky filled with many stars. Little Flower grew very tired and lay down to rest. Soon she fell deeply asleep. . . deeply into the time of Dreaming.

Soon Little Flower began to stir in her sleep. Her keen sense of smell awakened her to the familiar odor which she knew meant danger. Upon opening her sleep-filled brown eyes, she saw a great fire raging out of control. Her heart felt a big fear because she had no place to run. She felt helpless. She felt trapped.

As Little Flower stood trying to figure out a way to escape, the large white feather she had found earlier that day fell out of her fur. Little Flower picked it up with her mouth and suddenly she found herself being lifted higher and higher into the air until she was above the forest. . . above the fire.

Little Flower was able to see the fire in a very different way. She was not trapped anymore. . . she was safe.

As Little Flower flew higher and higher something strange began to happen. She realized that the great white feather was not in her mouth anymore. She wondered to herself, "How could I be flying without the feather? I am a deer, and deer cannot fly."

Just then she came across the Great White Eagle Mother sitting in the Mountain Cloud. "Hello," White Eagle Mother said, "thank you for bringing me my feather. You see, it dropped into your world while I was flying in my world. It was you who found my feather and it was you whom I blessed to bring it to me. Each of my feathers holds a prayer for all relatives of Earth. The prayer would have been lost forever, but it was you who found it. However, you in your deer form had no way of bringing it to me in my world, except through the Great Flight of changing forms. You had to cross the bridge from your world into mine. . . and I thank you. You are not just a deer anymore, but you, too, have become a great White Eagle Mother who will carry the prayers of all relatives within the feathers of your wings."

"And so, Little Flower, that is why the moon is white. . . . It is because the presence of all the White Eagle Mothers and Grandmothers show their faces in a great sacred council when the sky is dark and filled with stars. And, Little Flower, you are now one of the great White Eagle Mothers whose face will always be seen in the glow of the moon, and your heart's song will be carried with the breath of the wind."

■ ■ ■

Little Flower's heart was full, knowing that her question had been answered at last. As the woman finished her story, she looked up and saw that the sun had set. It was now the time of night and, through the mist of her warm tears, she noticed the brightness of the cloud-brushed moon. As if a flame had been lit to brighten an inner room of darkness, a smile began to emerge on her face bringing the gift of recognition . . . a recognition of someone close.

Table of Color Plates

▼

Joyce C. Mills has a Ph.D. in Clinical Psychology and is in private practice in Encino, California, where she is a consultant to medical, educational, private and media organizations. Specializing in storytelling for healing and Ericksonian Hypnotherapy, Dr. Mills presents her approaches both nationally and internationally on television and radio and has been published in numerous journals.

Dr. Mills is also co-author, with Richard J. Crowley, Ph.D., of Therapeutic Metaphors for Children and the Child Within, Cartoon Magic, and Sammy And Mr. Camel. Most recently, Dr. Mills is working on integrating Native American Teachings and Ericksonian Hypnotherapy and is on the Board of Directors of The Turtle Island Project.

Along with her busy life, Joyce is married to her husband Eddie and they have two sons, Todd and Casey.

Frank Howell, although holding numerous degrees in art and writing, considers himself to be a self-taught artist—drawing since he was a young child and painting for over thirty years. Mr. Howell's lyrical interpretation of his subject, be it an Indian face or a landscape, employs a visual imagery of the wind as it sweeps across time: past, present and future.

Howell's work has been widely exhibited at museums and galleries throughout the United States and is in numerous private and corporate collections.

In addition to being an accomplished artist, Mr. Howell is also a poet and writer, having recently completed two books, Frank Howell/Monotypes and Frank Howell/Lithographs.

Frank Howell lives and paints in Santa Fe, New Mexico, where he also owns the Frank Howell Gallery.

Mi Takuye Oyacin . . .

To All My Relations.